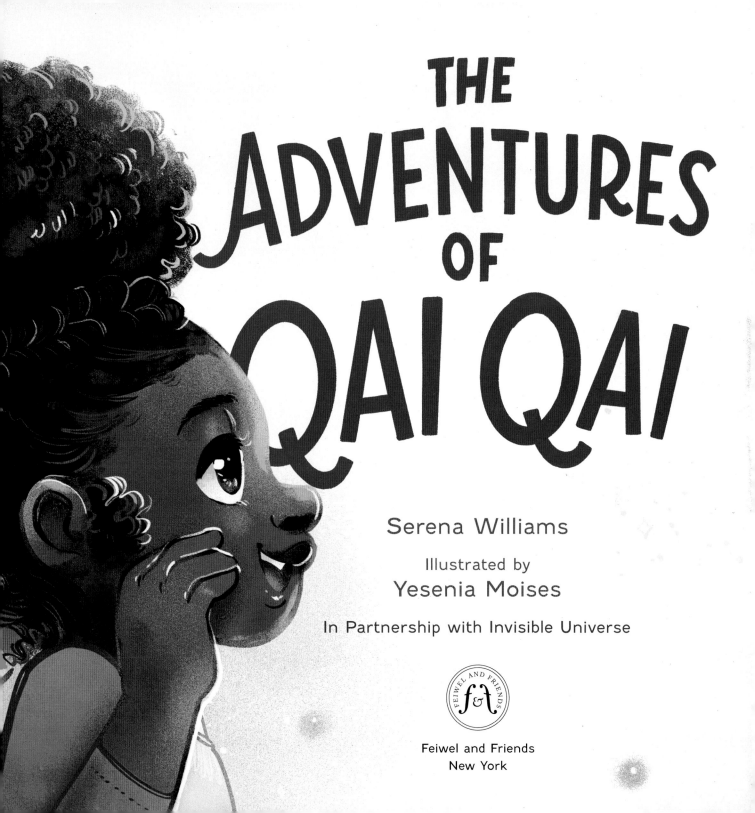

THE ADVENTURES OF QAI QAI

Serena Williams

Illustrated by
Yesenia Moises

In Partnership with Invisible Universe

Feiwel and Friends
New York

Baby Girl loves to prance, passé, and pirouette through her lovely home.

She twirls around Mama as she flips eggs in the kitchen.

She waltzes with Daddy as he sets the table for dinner. But most of all, Baby Girl dances with her best friend, and biggest fan, Qai Qai.

When Baby Girl improves her en pointe toe stand, Qai Qai's there to give her a high five.

When she needs a partner to practice the foxtrot with, she holds tight to Qai Qai's hands.

And when Baby Girl is nervous about her upcoming recital, Qai Qai's listening ears are always wide open.

"Qai," Baby Girl whispers under the starry night sky. "Tomorrow's the biggest day of my whole life. What if I forget the steps?"

Though Qai Qai's lips are glued shut, Baby Girl believes in her heart that her best friend is real.

"I know, I know. We've been practicing for weeks, but still, what happens if I freeze up there with so many people watching? I'm scared, Qai."

"Don't be scared, Best Friend!
I'm right here with you, always."

"But what if I'm not good enough?"

"Girl!" Qai Qai answers with her hands on her hips. "You're already good enough when you walk in the door! Come on, let me show you."

"Where are we going?"

"You're riding with Qai Qai now," she tells Baby Girl. "You need an outfit to match! Let's see what's in Mama's closet."

"Go ahead!
Pick something!
Anything you like!"
prompts Qai Qai.

"Look how it twirls, Qai Qai!"
"It's amazing!" Qai Qai agrees.
"I want to wear this, too!"

"You look perfect! You're ready for anything now!"

"Get it, Baby Girl!" Qai Qai shouts.
"Work that runway!"

"You see it, too, Qai?" asks Baby Girl.

"Of course I do!" she replies.
"Let's see what's on the other side
of that door."

Baby Girl looks up at the spotlight.
"Is this where I'll be performing
tomorrow?"

"Sure is," replies Qai Qai.

"It's SO huge, Qai Qai," says Baby Girl timidly. "It's the biggest stage I've ever danced on in my whole life. And I'll be the only one out there for my solo."

"You believed in me," says Qai Qai.
"The power of your belief brought me to life. Now you need to believe in yourself. Trust your instincts and let your bright light shine! Step out there on that stage and do your thing. And, Baby Girl, you're never alone. I've always got your back!"

"Today's the day," Daddy says as he ties Baby Girl's dance shoes.

"We'll be front and center watching you, Baby Girl," Mama says. "You'll be amazing."

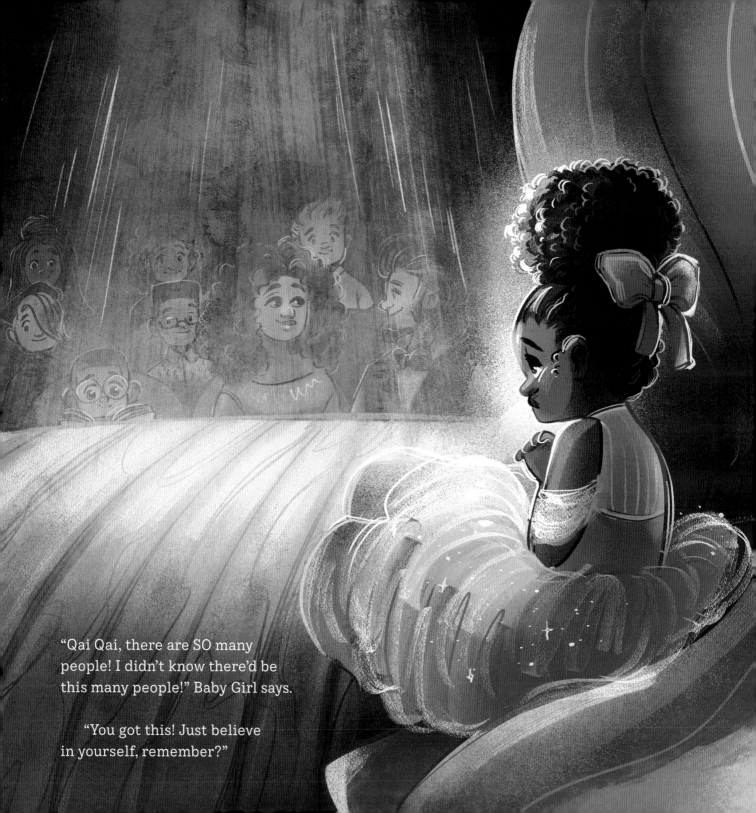

"Qai Qai, there are SO many
people! I didn't know there'd be
this many people!" Baby Girl says.

"You got this! Just believe
in yourself, remember?"

"Can you come with me?"

"Baby Girl, you don't need me to. I'm always with you. That's how best friends work!"

"I believe in myself,"
Baby Girl says with her chin
high in the air. "I'm ready!"

"That was awesome!" Baby Girl shouts joyfully.
"I didn't fall! Or forget any of the steps!"

"Not only did you not fall," says Daddy, "you leaped so high into the air, it looked like you were flying."

"Like a beautiful bird!" Mama adds. "We knew you could do it. Never had a single doubt."

"Great job, Best Friend. I knew you could do it, too," Qai Qai whispers so Mama and Daddy can't hear.

"What should we do next, Qai?"

"Anything you want, Baby Girl.
You can do anything!"

This book is dedicated to all little girls.
Let this book be a constant reminder that you
can do anything you put your mind to.
Imagine it, believe it, do it.

—SERENA

A Feiwel and Friends Book
An imprint of Macmillan Publishing Group, LLC
120 Broadway, New York, NY 10271
mackids.com

Our books may be purchased in bulk for promotional, educational, or business use.
Please contact your local bookseller or the Macmillan Corporate and Premium Sales Department at
(800) 221-7945 ext. 5442 or by email at MacmillanSpecialMarkets@macmillan.com.

Library of Congress Cataloging-in-Publication Data is available.

First edition, 2022
Book design by Mike Burroughs
The artwork for this book was created with Adobe Photoshop
using Kyle T Webster's brushes on a Wacom Cintiq Pro 24.
Feiwel and Friends logo designed by Filomena Tuosto
Printed in China by RR Donnelley Asia Printing Solutions Ltd., Dongguan City, Guangdong Province

ISBN 978-1-250-83140-8 (hardcover)
1 3 5 7 9 10 8 6 4 2